Kindest

Susannah McFarlane   Lachlan Creagh

A Scholastic Australia Book

This is Katie with some of her friends—
Kylie, Ken, Kai and Kayla.

Katie is kind. She is the kindest
koala in the whole kindergarten
and in all the Kimberley.

Katie helps Kai with his karate
and kickboxing.

Katie keeps Ken, a keen cook, company in the kitchen. They are making a feast for the upcoming Kimberley Karaoke Competition.

There are kumquats with ketchup and kiwifruit kebabs!

Katie kicks back with
Kayla in her kennel under
the kurrajong tree.

Katie and Kayla knit
knickerbockers for the
karaoke competitors.

On the day of the competition,
something kooky happened . . .

The Kimberley karaoke machine was knocked over.

Kaboom!

It was kaput!

With no karaoke machine, there would be no Kimberley Karaoke Competition. Everyone had their knickerbockers in a knot. No kidding!

Katie kept calm and carried on.
She took knives, knots and other
knick-knacks out of her khaki
kitbag and got cracking.

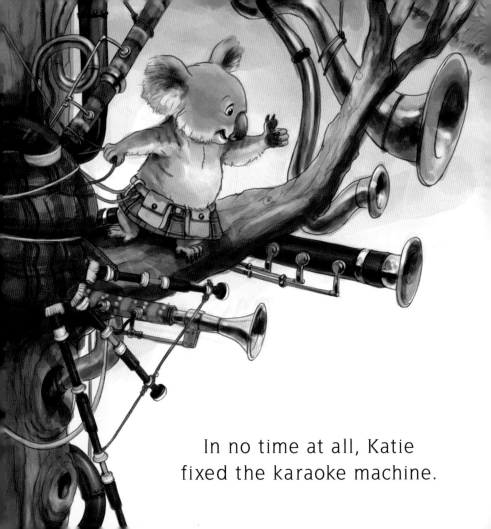

In no time at all, Katie
fixed the karaoke machine.

Kind *and* clever—what a koala!

The karaoke competition
kicked on all through the night!

Five lit-tle jo-eys
jump-ing on the bed . . .

That's Katie kitted out in the kimono.

Kai was crowned the
Kimberley Karaoke King.
Katie and all the Kimberley
crew congratulated Kai.
What a cracker of a night!

Good on you Katie (and Kylie, Ken, Kai and Kayla).

What about you?
Are you kind too?